Dedicated to my son, Cody
(My Codybear Always),
For whom this book was written.
And to my two beautiful granddaughters,
Skylar and Emma.

A very special thank you to Joseph Fritts
for helping me accomplish my Biggest dreams
of publishing this book.
Thank You, My Wonderful Joe, Baby!

Edited by editorShirley@fiverr.com
Illustrations by ValentinArt | Designed by MediaMetiers
Written by Angela Dunn

Hi, my name is Constantia!
I am a tooth fairy in training.
I work hard every day in the
classroom so that I can be the
best tooth fairy I can possibly be!

On graduation day, all graduating fairies like myself are given a tooth fairy signal. It's a little purple light with a built-in location device. It automatically sends us right on our way to where we need to be.

The purple fairy light signal is about the size of a pea. Since I am not much bigger, I wear it around my neck as a necklace so as not to lose it.

When a child loses a tooth or teeth, in some cases, my purple light flashes and beeps ever so lightly as not to disturb sleeping children. Then, we collect the tooth or teeth that set off our beeps. It is our job as fairies to replace the tooth or teeth with a treasure.

Well, about three long nights ago, my tooth fairy signal flashed and beeped in its light purple glow.

Oh, how excited I was!
It was my first ever tooth collecting
adventure! With its built-in
location device, there was no
guessing where to be or how
to get there. I hurried just as
fast as I could, which is pretty fast!
We fairies travel almost at the
speed of light!

When I arrived at your house,
I crept through your window
ever so gently.
Then onto your bed, and I started
looking under your pillow for
that tooth that had set off my beep.

I looked on the floor because
sometimes that's where the
tooth can be.
I looked high, and I looked low.
I looked all around your room.
But alas, I could not
find that tooth that had set
off my beep!

In my despair,
I started second-guessing my
tooth fairy signal.
I thought maybe it was on
the bleep? I thought,
maybe in all my rush and
excitement, I had visited
the wrong house.

I pondered, and I thought,
"What could be wrong with
me?" I even left your room as
to not disturb you.
But then, I remembered I am
Constantia, the tooth fairy,
and that this is my trained
specialty! No tooth fairy's
signal has ever been wrong
before. Not ever!

So, I tried this one last time for that tooth of yours, the tooth that would soon be mine! I crept back into your room, in search of that missing tooth, without disturbing you.

I climbed back onto your bed;
I tripped and stumbled; I
couldn't catch my landing,
and I fell right into your head!
And to my surprise, what did I see?
That big hole where that tooth used to be!!

I knew for certain there would be no more searching. I had seen all I needed to see! And ever so silently, I left a special treasure for you under your pillow. My tooth fairy senses tell me that I will see you again, soon!

The End!

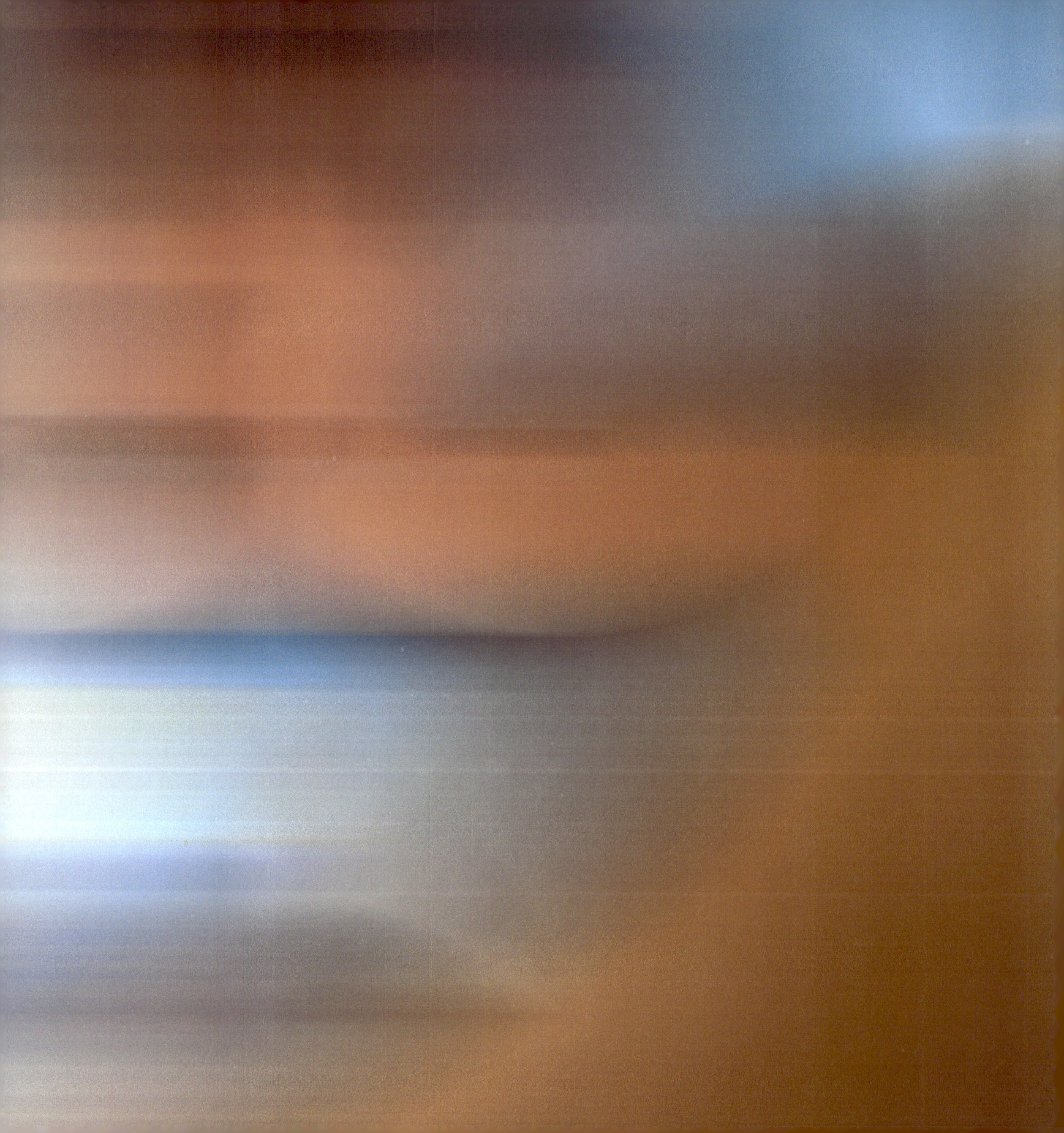